SHAPES & SIZES

Pedro & Pete

BY BOBBY BASIL

3 FREE BOOKS!

Go to bobbybasilwriter.com!

BASIC SPANISH PHRASES

Pedro & Pete

¡Hola!

Hello!

BY BOBBY BASIL

DAYS & MONTHS
Pedro & Pete

Lunes

Monday

BY BOBBY BASIL

Pedro & Pete have more books!

- **Counting Numbers**
- **Colors**
- **Family**
- **Clothing**
- **Food**
- **Animals**
- **Weather & Seasons**
- **Household Items**
- **Transportation**
- **School Supplies**

3 FREE BOOKS!

Go to bobbybasilwriter.com!

Made in the USA
Middletown, DE
29 January 2019